Three Scoops and a Fig

For Cal, Olivia, and Grace, with all my love
—S. L. A.

For Steve & Jessica
—S. K. H.

Published by
PEACHTREE PUBLISHERS
1700 Chattahoochee Avenue
Atlanta, Georgia 30318-2112
www.peachtree-online.com

Book design by Melanie McMahon Ives

Illustrations created in watercolor on archival quality 100% rag watercolor paper

Printed in May 2010 by Imago in Singapore
10 9 8 7 6 5 4 3 2 1
First Edition

Library of Congress Cataloging-in-Publication Data

Akin, Sara.
  Three scoops and a fig / written by Sara Laux Akin ; illustrated by Susan Kathleen Hartung.
     p. cm.
  Summary: Tired of always being told she is too little to help in the busy kitchen of her family's Italian restaurant, Sofia is inspired by a storm and a fig tree to come up with a delicious recipe of her own. Includes facts about the foods mentioned in the story.
  ISBN 978-1-56145-522-5 / 1-56145-522-9
  [1. Cookery, Italian--Fiction. 2. Restaurants--Fiction. 3. Family life--Fiction.] I. Hartung, Susan Kathleen, ill. II. Title.
  PZ7.A311Th 2010
  [E]--dc22
            2009024519

Three Scoops and a Fig

written by Sara Laux Akin

illustrated by Susan Kathleen Hartung

Ω

PEACHTREE
ATLANTA

Scrumptious smells tickled Sofia's nose, stirring her from sleep.

"Figaro, do I smell spaghetti sauce?"

Her little cat wiggled his whiskers.

"Everyone must be cooking already," Sofia said. "I want to make something special for Nonno and Nonna, too."

She threw on her favorite dress and ran downstairs to the kitchen of her family's restaurant. Figaro followed at her heels.

Papa was chopping garlic on a big butcher's block.

"Will Nonno and Nonna be here soon?" Sofia asked.

"Good morning, Olive Eyes," Papa said. "Your grandparents should arrive before The Fig Tree opens for dinner."

"Nonna says kings would trade their crowns for a spoonful of your sauce, Papa," Sofia said. "I'll help you make it!"

She pushed a button on the blender.

Whirrrrr! Splotches of tomato sauce sailed to the ceiling.

Figaro hid under the table.

"Mamma mia!" shouted Papa. *"Bambina, sei troppo piccola!"*

Sofia's cheeks burned. "I am *not* too little!" she cried.

Sofia ran outside and climbed high into her favorite fig

tree. It was dotted with ripe fruit. She nestled into its branches

the way she always nestled into Nonno's lap.

Soon the warm smell of bread floated up and out of a

nearby window.

Sofia hurried back into the kitchen.

Mama was putting a pan of breadsticks in the oven.

"Nonna says that queens would curtsey for a bite of your bread, Mama," Sofia said. "I'll help you make it!"

"You can measure yeast into that bowl on the counter," Mama said. "Only two tablespoons."

Oops! Sofia had already poured five tablespoons of yeast into the bowl. Maybe six.

Sofia and Figaro played under the table. After a while, Sofia peeked at the dough rising in the warm oven. Up, up, up! The yeasty dough was swelling over the bowl like a giant marshmallow!

"Mamma mia!" Mama shouted. "Too much yeast! *Bambina, sei troppo piccola!*"

Sofia's eyes prickled with tears. "I am *not* too little!" she cried.

She ran back outside and
sat beneath her fig tree, tossing
breadcrumbs to the finches.

She hoped Nonna and Nonno
would hurry. She missed the feel of
Nonna's hands smoothing her hair
and the sound of Nonno's voice
telling her Italian folktales.

"*Ciao,* Sofia!" her brother Mario
called as he came around the corner.
He was carrying a bag of fresh
vegetables. "Time for me to fly
some pizza pies."

Sofia jumped up. "Nonna says that princes and princesses would sell their ponies for a piece of your pizza," she said. "I'll help you make it!"

She followed Mario into the kitchen and grabbed an apron from the hook. "Watch this!" she said.

She tossed a ball of pizza dough high in the air, just like Mario.

Splat! It caught in the ceiling fan.

"Mamma mia!" Mario shouted. *"Sei troppo piccola!"*

Sofia's lip quivered. "I am *not* too little!" she cried.

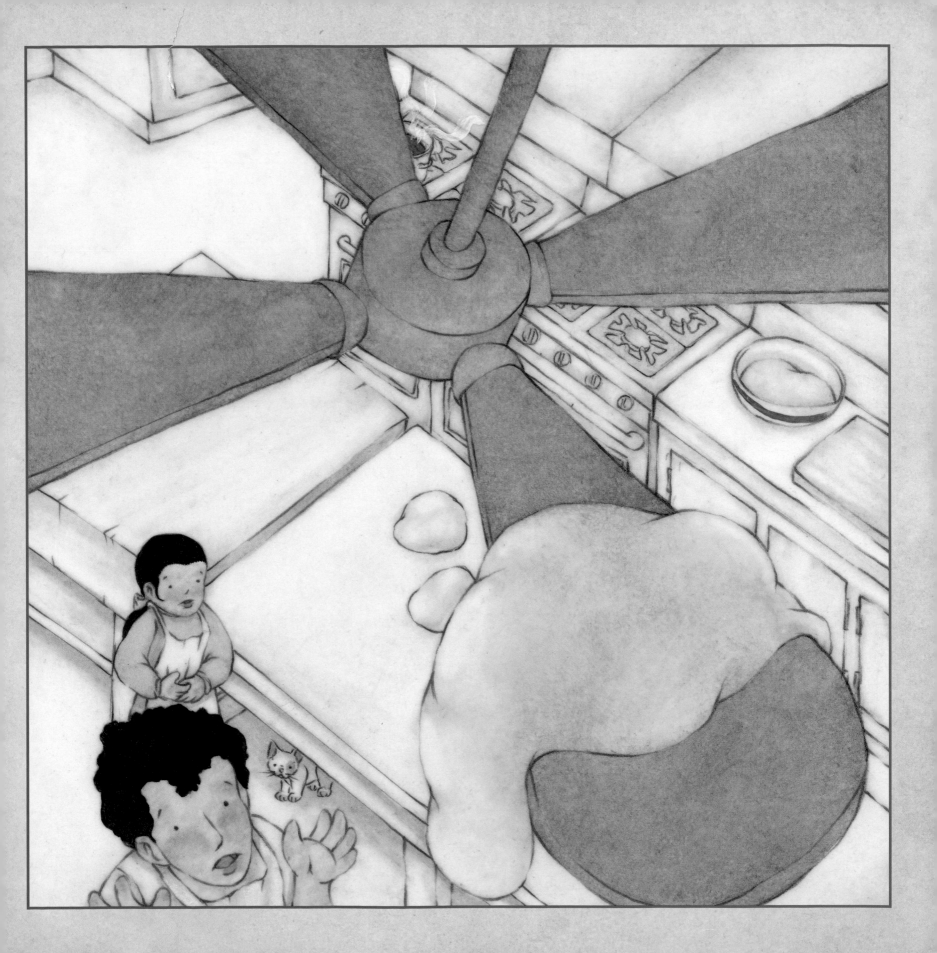

Water hissed in pots on the stove.

Papa chopped, Mama baked, and

Mario tossed. Nobody wanted Sofia's help.

With a sigh, she went to the freezer and

scooped up two bowls of Italian ice cream. Papa, Mama,

and Mario were busy. No one would notice if she and Figaro

had gelato for breakfast.

Sofia took the bowls outside.

Raindrops began to sprinkle her face.

She sat on the swing under her

favorite tree. Its big, leafy branches

made a fig tree umbrella.

Whoosh! A strong wind tousled

Sofia's hair.

Whoosh! Whoosh! Figaro jumped

into the swing and cuddled close

beside her.

Whoosh! Plop! A fat, juicy fig fell

into Sofia's bowl.

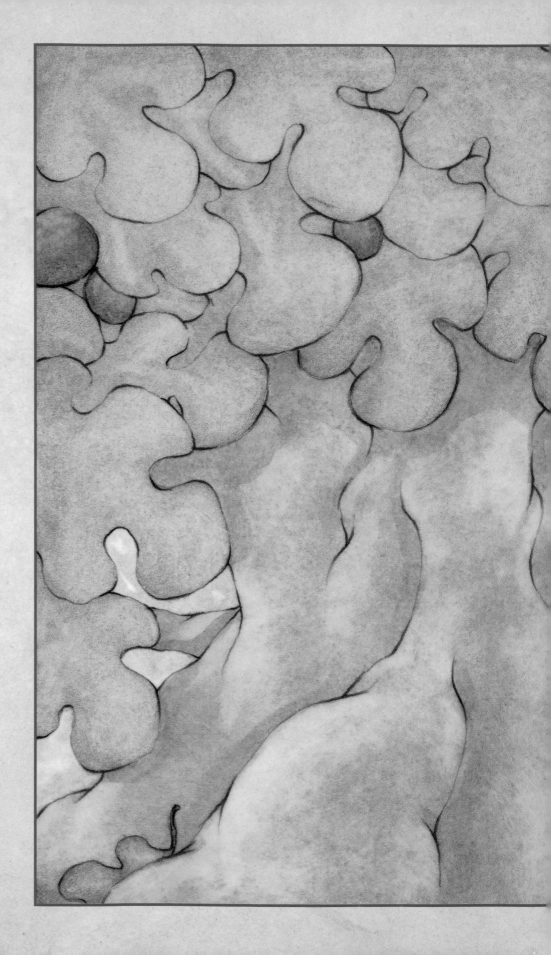

Sofia picked up the gelato-covered fig and

licked it like an ice cream cone.

"Mamma mia!" she shouted. "This is delicious!"

Figaro thought so, too.

Sofia jumped off the swing. "I have an idea," she told Figaro. Quickly she gathered the ripe figs the wind had scattered on the ground. Then she ran to the kitchen, the skirt of her dress brimming with beautiful fruit.

Sofia dumped the little pear-shaped figs into a bowl on the table. She dished out more helpings of gelato, each with three scoops and a fig.

Knock, knock.

Nonno and Nonna were here!

"Ciao, bella," Nona said, giving Sofia a hug. "Look at the lovely figs you found."

"Come and try my specialty," Sofia said. "There's enough for everyone."

"Fantastico!" said Papa, taking a bite. "Sofia, you've created a delicious dessert for our menu: Sofia's Fig Tree Sundae!"

"Squisito!" said Mama. "Three scoops for three generations of our family."

"And a fig for Figaro," Mario added.

"Brava, piccolina!" said Nonno. "Good job!"

Nonna licked her spoon. "Angels would sing for one of your Fig Tree Sundaes, Sofia!"

Sofia skipped outside and wrapped

her arms around the old fig tree.

"Grazie," she whispered. "Thank you."

All over the world, stories and recipes are shared from one generation to the next, just like in Sofia's family. Many people believe that Italian folktales were among the first to be recorded in written form. These stories often included royal families.

In one such tale, "The King's Daughter Who Could Never Get Enough Figs," a princess had such a great love of figs that her father didn't know what to do. The king finally promised his subjects that the young man who succeeded in giving his daughter her fill of figs could marry her!

❦

Here is a variation of Sofia's special Fig Tree Sundae for you to try. The three flavors of gelato, which is Italy's version of ice cream, create the colors of the Italian flag: green, white, and red.

If you wish, you can substitute ice cream for the gelato.

Italian Flag Sundae

1 scoop mint or pistachio gelato
1 scoop vanilla gelato
1 scoop strawberry or cherry gelato

Top with a fig!

The full story of "The King's Daughter Who Could Never Get Enough Figs" can be found in ITALIAN FOLKTALES by Italo Calvino (English translation copyright Harcourt Books, 1980).

Italian words and phrases from THREE SCOOPS AND A FIG

nonno—grandfather (NOHN-noh)

nonna—grandmother (NOHN-nah)

mamma mia!—oh, my! (MAHM-mah MEE-ah)

bambina, sei troppo piccola—child, you are too little

      (bahm-BEE-nah, say TROH-poh PEEK-koh-lah)

ciao—hello (chow)

ciao, bella—hello, beautiful (chow, BELL-ah)

fantastico—fantastic (fahn-TAHS-tee-koh)

squisito—exquisite (skwee-ZEE-toh)

brava, piccolina—excellent, little one (BRAH-vah, peek-koh-LEE-nah)

grazie—thank you (GRAH-tsee-eh)

The author would like to thank the people at Casa Italia Italian Cultural Center in Stone Park, Illinois, for their gracious assistance with the Italian phrases. And she extends a special *grazie* to Lisa Mathews.